A HAUNTED HOUSE STORYBOOK

THE HAUNTED ELEVATOR

BY RICK DETORIE

Watermill Press

For
Tara

Randa lived with her mom and dad on the third floor of a thirteen-story apartment building. Their apartment was small. Because her parents slept in the one tiny bedroom, Randa had to sleep every night on the lumpy old couch in the living room.

In Randa's apartment building there were three elevators, two on one side of the hall, and one on the other side. Randa liked riding on the elevators, and usually hopped on the first one to open when she pressed the shiny glass buttons.

One day, Randa's mother said to her, "Randa, I don't want you to use that elevator anymore." She pointed to the elevator across the hall. "You may ride on these two, but not that one."

"Why not, Mama?" said Randa.

"I have my reasons," said her mother mysteriously. "Just stay out of that elevator, please."

For the next few days Randa avoided the third elevator, but she was so bothered by not knowing why she should stay off that elevator, that she decided to ask her friend Jilly about it. Jilly was very smart. She knew how to ride a two-wheeler, how to draw a five-pointed star, and how to make Mrs. Gillespie's cat talk like a baby. If anyone would know the secret of the third elevator, Jilly would.

"Randa!" screamed Jilly as she opened her door. "You're just in time! I need a maid of honor!"

"Jilly, I don't have time to play royal wedding with you today," said Randa. "I have something more important to talk to you about."

Then Randa told Jilly what her mother had said about the elevator.

7

"Hah!" said Jilly. "I know why your mother doesn't like that elevator! It's haunted!"

"Haunted?" gasped Randa.

"Sure, and I can prove it," said Jilly. "Follow me."

Jilly led Randa down the hall to the third elevator and pushed the button. The door opened.

"I can't ride in it," said Randa. "I promised my mom!"

"We're not going for a ride," said Jilly. "We're just going to peek inside!"

"Look," said Jilly, pointing to the buttons with numbers on them. "Do you see that top number?"

"Thirteen," said Randa.

"Yes, this is the only elevator in the building that has that number," said Jilly. "It's the only elevator that goes to that floor!"

"So?" said Randa.

"So?" shouted Jilly. "Don't you know what that means? It means this elevator is haunted! Let's get out of here!"

The girls ran down the hall and crept under the staircase, where Jilly told Randa the story of the haunted elevator.

"Once upon a time," said Jilly, "a little boy named Hans got on a haunted elevator and pressed the number five button, but the elevator didn't stop at five."

"Instead, the lights went out and Hans was zoomed up to the thirteenth floor in the dark. There, the doors opened and before he knew what was happening, a horrible zombie monster grabbed and turned him into a shrunken head. The end."

"Oh, Jilly," laughed Randa. "Wherever did you get such a silly story?"

"In a Creepy Comic Book," said Jilly, "so it must be true!"

That night in bed Randa thought about Jilly's story. She didn't exactly believe the story, but Randa couldn't think of another good reason why her mother would want her to stay off that elevator.

The next afternoon, Randa and Jilly decided to watch from
the lobby to see if any zombie-type monsters got on or off the
haunted elevator.

"Look!" whispered Jilly. "There's one!"

"That doesn't look like a zombie monster to me," said Randa.
"It looks like an ordinary workman carrying an ordinary lunch
pail." "A lunch pail filled with shrunken heads," hissed Jilly.

A few days passed and Randa forgot about the haunted elevator until one morning when her mother said, "Randa dear, come with me, please. I want to show you something."

Randa held her mother's hand as her mom led her to the haunted elevator and pushed the up button. The door opened and her mother stepped inside.

"Well, come on, Randa," her mother said.

"But, Mama," said Randa, "you told me not to ride in this . . . this elevator!"

"Yes," said her mother, "and now you'll see why I told you not to."

Randa was shaking with fear as her mother pushed button number thirteen. Oh, no, thought Randa, maybe her mother had become a zombie monster!

The haunted elevator rose to the thirteenth floor and stopped. The doors slid open.

"Mama, Mama, the lights went out," cried Randa. "I can't see!"

"That's because your eyes are closed," said Randa's mother. "Open them up and look!"

Randa slowly opened her eyes. There, through the elevator door, she saw not a zombie monster, but her dad standing next to an open doorway.

"Surprise!" shouted her mother and father.

"It's our big new apartment," said her dad. "It's on the top floor! Not only do you get your own bedroom, but you get your very own playroom as well!"

Randa was so surprised, she didn't know what to say.

"Now you know why I told you not to use this elevator," said Randa's mother. "I didn't want you coming up here before the workmen were finished fixing it up. It would have spoiled the surprise!"

Everyone liked the big new apartment, including Jilly who
started to ride on the "haunted elevator" all the time.